Happy Adoption Day!

For the Jocking family.....
Rachel, Dom, Christian & Tayra
With love from The Magnants

ption Day!

Lyrics by
John McCutcheon

Illustrations by
Julie Paschkis

LITTLE, BROWN AND COMPANY

New York ☙ Boston

Little, Brown and Company

Time Warner Book Group
1271 Avenue of the Americas, New York, NY 10020
Visit our Web site at www.lb-kids.com

First Edition

From the recording *Family Garden* (Rounder Records 8026)

Library of Congress Cataloging-in-Publication Data

McCutcheon, John.
    Happy Adoption Day! / lyrics by John McCutcheon ; illustrations by Julie Paschkis — 1st ed.
      p. cm.
    Summary: Parents celebrate the day on which they adopted their child and continue to reassure the new
addition to their family that it is wanted, loved, and very special.
    ISBN 0-316-55455-3 (hc) / 0-316-60323-6 (pb)
    1. Children's songs — Texts.   [1. Adoption — Songs and music.   2. Family life — Songs and music.
3. Songs.]   I. Paschkis, Julie, ill.   II. Title.
PZ8.3.M459545Hap 1996
782.42 — dc20   95-41643

HC: 10 9 8 7 6
PB: 10 9 8 7 6 5 4 3

IM

The paintings for this book were done in gouache on Arches watercolor paper.

Printed and bound in China

To my mother, Abby McCutcheon,
who brought so many families together via
adoption
—J. M.

To my sister, Janet Lord
—J. P.

Oh, who would have guessed? Who could have seen?

Who could have possibly known?

All these roads we have traveled, the places we've been

Would have finally taken us home?

There are those who think families happen by chance,
A mystery their whole life through,
But we had a voice and we had a choice —
We were working and waiting for you.

So it's here's to you and three cheers to you!
Let's shout it, "Hip, hip, hip, hooray!"
For out of a world so tattered and torn,
You came to our house on that wonderful morn . . .

And all of a sudden this family was born. Oh, happy Adoption Day!

Wherever you came from, wherever you go,
This is the place that we start.

Whatever you learn, whoever you know,
You've still got a home in our hearts.

Some parents come different, some come the same,
But whether they're single or pairs,

You're never alone, you're always at home
Whenever there's love we can share.

So it's here's to you and three cheers to you!

Let's shout it, "Hip, hip, hip, hooray!"

For out of a world so tattered and torn,

You came to our house on that wonderful morn,

And all of a sudden this family was born.

Oh, happy Adoption Day!

No matter the name and no matter the age,
No matter how you came to be,

No matter the skin, we are all of us kin—
We are all of us one family.

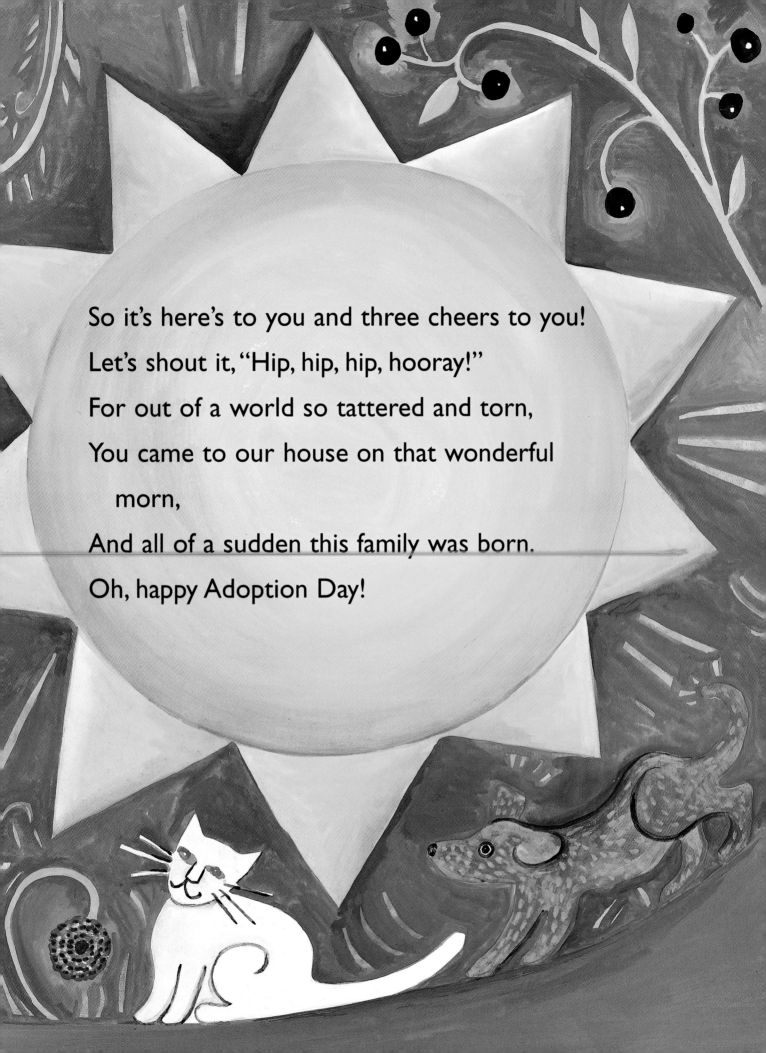

So it's here's to you and three cheers to you!

Let's shout it, "Hip, hip, hip, hooray!"

For out of a world so tattered and torn,

You came to our house on that wonderful

   morn,

And all of a sudden this family was born.

Oh, happy Adoption Day!

Happy Adoption Day!

Words and Music by John McCutcheon

From the recording *Family Garden* (Rounder Records 8026)